# The Kids in Mrs. Z's Class
## The Legend of Memo Castillo

# The **Kids** in Mrs. Z's Class
## The Legend of Memo Castillo

**WILLIAM ALEXANDER**

illustrated by **KAT FAJARDO**

Series coordinated by Kate Messner

ALGONQUIN YOUNG READERS
WORKMAN PUBLISHING
NEW YORK

Copyright © 2024 by William Alexander
Illustrations copyright © 2024 by Kat Fajardo
Cover art color and interior shading by Pablo A. Castro
Kraft paper texture © klyaksun/Shutterstock

Algonquin Young Readers
Workman Publishing
Hachette Book Group, Inc.
1290 Avenue of the Americas
New York, NY 10104
workman.com

Algonquin Young Readers is an imprint of Workman Publishing, a division of Hachette Book Group, Inc. The Workman name and logo are registered trademarks of Hachette Book Group, Inc.

Design by Neil Swaab

The publisher is not responsible for websites (or their content) that are not owned by the publisher.

Workman books may be purchased in bulk for business, educational, or promotional use. For information, please contact your local bookseller or the Hachette Book Group Special Markets Department at special.markets@hbgusa.com.

Library of Congress Cataloging-in-Publication Data is available.
ISBN 978-1-5235-2747-2 (hardcover)
ISBN 978-1-5235-2748-9 (paperback)

First Edition October 2024 LSC-C
Printed in Indiana, USA, on responsibly sourced paper.

10 9 8 7 6 5 4 3 2 1

*For the kids who came from Atlantis and Krypton*

# MEET
# The Kids in Mrs. Z's Class

Adam

Ayana

Carlota

Emma

# Chapter 1

# A Game of Sorcery

The legend of Memo Castillo began with a game of cards.

It was Saturday, and almost dinnertime. Memo sat on the floor of his room, broken leg resting on a pillow. His ankle itched under the cast. He tried to ignore the itch. He had more important things to focus on, because Theo had just thrown a lightning bolt at him.

"Zap!" Theo said. "You lose four points."

"Ow," Memo said.

"This game is confusing," Wyatt said.

"You'll get the hang of it," said Memo. "Watch this. I'm going to attack him with an army of bunnies!"

He played a card with a picture of sword-swinging rabbit warriors on it.

Memo and Theo were teaching Wyatt how to play Sorcery—a game with a bazillion different kinds of collectible cards. Each card was a magic spell like "Throw Lightning Bolt" or "Summon Ferocious Rabbits." Playing the game was like fighting a magical duel.

"Can I cast my own lightning bolt?" Wyatt asked.

"Nope," Theo said. "You do not have enough crystals."

Wyatt frowned at his cards. "This game is *really* confusing."

Memo, Theo, and Wyatt were all classmates

at Curiosity Academy. It was a new school this year, so Memo didn't really know most of the other kids. He did know Theo, though. They had been best friends since kindergarten, when they tried to invent time travel with juice boxes.

Wyatt was a new friend. He sometimes sat at the dragon table during school lunch, so Memo had invited him to join their Saturday Sorcery game. Wyatt didn't seem to be having very much fun, though. He put down his cards.

"You two should finish the game without me," Wyatt said. "Can I draw something on your cast?"

"Sure," Memo said.

Wyatt took a marker from his backpack and started to draw a purple dragon on Memo's ankle, which still itched. Memo held his breath and tried to make the itch go away. It didn't work.

"How did you hurt your leg?" Wyatt asked.

"I was reading," Memo said.

"Really?" Wyatt asked. "Was it a dangerous book?"

"He tried to read in a tree," Theo explained. "Then he fell asleep, fell out of the tree, and broke his leg in four places."

"Ouch," Wyatt said while trying not to laugh.

"Maybe the tree was mad about the book?" Theo wondered. "Books are made of paper. Paper is made out of trees. This tree probably rocked him to sleep on purpose. Then it tossed him to the ground."

Memo threw a pillow at Theo and missed.

"It's your turn," Memo said, "and we need

to practice for the tournament. Cast your next spell!"

"What tournament?" Wyatt asked.

"The GREAT SORCERY TOURNAMENT at MagiCon," Theo announced.

Wyatt still looked a little bit lost. "Magi-what?"

"It's a big gathering of geeks," Memo explained.

"It is so much more than that!" Theo said. "We went to the MagiCon convention last year, and it was amazing. My dad was one of the volunteers. All sorts of science fiction and fantasy stuff got packed into one building in the city. They had costumes and comics and authors and actors and NASA engineers answering everybody's silly questions."

"And a Sorcery tournament," Memo added,

"which Theo and I are *absolutely* going to win this year."

"We'll play as a team," Theo said.

"We'll cast powerful spells," Memo said.

"And we will defeat last year's champion, Josh Harkan," Theo swore.

"Is he that fifth grader who dresses like a vampire?" Wyatt asked.

"That's him," Memo said. "Do you want to come with us?"

"You'll need a costume," Theo pointed out. "I plan to be a cyborg. Half human, half robot."

"I'll be an elf," Memo said.

"Sounds fun," Wyatt said, though he looked like he didn't really want to join a great big gathering of costumed geekery.

"It's still your turn," Memo said to Theo. "Cast your spell, Sorcerer!"

## Chapter 2

# The Song of the Itch

Theo played "Nightmare Stampede" to scare away Memo's army of bunnies. The picture on the card showed horses galloping across the night sky.

Memo cast "The Ballad of the Exiled Queen" to give the bunnies enough courage to resist the nightmares. The picture showed an elf with a crown and long white hair.

"What does the name mean?" Wyatt asked.

"A *ballad* is a song that's also a story,"

Memo said, "and *exiled* means that you left your home and can't go back."

Theo grinned. "And now you have to sing, Memo! Every time you cast a spell with a song in it, you have to make up a song to go with it."

"Really?" Wyatt asked. He finished drawing the purple dragon and wrote "Wyvern the Magnificent" underneath.

"Really," Theo said.

Memo didn't want to sing. He'd hoped that Theo had forgotten about that rule. No such luck, though. Theo's memory was amazing. He knew all of his favorite movies by heart.

Memo's friends waited for him to make up a ballad about an exiled elf queen, right there, on the spot. Memo was pretty good at that sort of thing. He made up little songs all the time. Still, the whole idea of singing in front of other people—even his friends—made his entire body feel just as itchy as his ankle. But that was how the game was played. He cast the spell, so he had to sing. He cleared his throat.

Then the door opened wide and scattered Sorcery cards across the floor. An old woman with long white hair stood in the doorway. Memo thought that she looked like an elf queen.

"Hi, Lala," he said.

"Lala" was short for "abuela," which meant "grandmother" in Spanish.

She glanced down at the scattered cards and winced. She seemed embarrassed to have messed up the game. Then she said something that Memo couldn't understand. He caught a couple of English words like "time"

and "game," but the rest was a blur of Spanish that all smooshed together.

She nodded once and left.

"What did she say?" Theo asked.

"That it's almost time for dinner?" Memo guessed. He hated to admit that he couldn't really speak Spanish.

"Theo!" a voice called from downstairs. "Wyatt! Time to go!"

". . . and that Theo's mom is here," Memo added.

That was the end of the game. Theo's mom was going to drive Wyatt home, so both of them had to leave.

Wyatt grabbed his backpack. "Thanks for inviting me," he mumbled.

Theo gathered up his scattered cards. "Your dad knows that he is driving us to the convention next week, right?" he said to Memo.

"Right," Memo said.

"Double-check with him, okay?" Theo said.

"I will," Memo promised.

"Because he sometimes forgets things like that," Theo said. "Probably because he does not get any sleep now that you have a new baby sister. And my parents are busy next Saturday, so we really need your dad to remember this time. We need an adult to sponsor us for the tournament."

"Don't worry about it," Memo said.

"And do not forget about our Sorcery practice tomorrow after school," Theo said. "We need to be ready!"

"I'll be there," Memo said.

"Theeeeeeeooooooooooooo!"

Theo and Wyatt scrambled downstairs.

"Bye!" Memo called after them.

His ankle still fiercely itched beneath the cast.

He sang a song of annoyance at it.

*"Go away itch,*
*go away itch,*
*my foot isn't itchy anymooooooooore . . ."*

The song worked like a magic spell. The itch disappeared.

Memo grinned, grabbed his crutches, and went downstairs for dinner.

# Chapter 3
# The Elvish Feast

Dinner smelled like stewed joy.

The rest of the family had already gathered in the kitchen, where they helped themselves to spoonfuls of rice, fried plantains, and ropa vieja (which means "old clothes" in Spanish, because the meat simmers on the stove long enough to fall apart like a pair of ripped jeans). Everybody was talking at once—Lala, Mom, Dad, and all four of Memo's sisters. (He was right in the middle, with two older sisters and two younger ones.) All of their voices danced over and around each other.

Memo stood in the doorway and listened to the happy noise for a moment. He imagined that the kitchen was really a feasting hall in a fantasy kingdom of elves. Their family name was Castillo, which meant "castle" in Spanish, so it felt right to pretend that all of them lived in a castle.

Dad was obviously an elf king. He held the baby Princess Ana against his shoulder and tried to get her to burp with gentle pats of his hand.

Princess Ana babbled instead of burping. Maybe her baby talk meant something secret and powerful. Maybe she was really casting her own kind of spells.

Four-year-old Princess Dina sat in her high-chair throne and demanded rice. Queen Mom

scooped rice onto Dina's plate while talking about a video meeting of royal counselors that took up her whole day, even though it was Saturday.

Mari and Neida—Memo's two older sisters—leaned close and whispered secrets to each other. Memo decided that they were royal spies rather than princesses. Both of them would probably agree.

*Am I a prince in this story?* he wondered. *Maybe I got wounded in battle. Or maybe I hurt my leg by trying to read a book while riding a horse.*

Lala hummed to herself while dropping pots and pans into the sink.

*She's a queen in exile,* Memo thought. *Just like on the card. She comes from a lost island kingdom.*

That was sort of true. The Castillo family came from Cuba, which is an island in the Caribbean. Memo's parents didn't talk about

Cuba very much. They left the island before they had kids, and none of them ever went back to visit. (Lala—Dad's mom—came to visit them in the United States instead. Then she never went back, either.) Memo had never seen Cuba except in pictures. It felt more like a legend than a real place.

Dina noticed him standing in the doorway. "Memo!" she shouted. "Sit here!"

Memo put his crutches in the corner and hopped to the empty kitchen chair right next to Dina.

"You're a frog," Dina told him.

"Ribbit," Memo said.

Dina bopped his nose to turn him from a frog back into a prince.

Lala was the last member of the family to sit down at the table. She lifted her fork like a golden wand.

The feast began. It was yummy. Memo tried to remember to chew, but shoveling food into his mouth felt much more important than chewing.

"More rice!" Dina demanded.

"Practice your Spanish," Mom told her. "Arroz."

"A rose?" Dina asked.

"Arroz by any other name would taste as sweet," Dad said. Then he laughed. (He was the only one who laughed.)

"Arroz means rice," Mom said to Dina. "Can you roll the *R* with the tip of your tongue when you say it?"

Dina tried, but she just sputtered and spit some of her chewed-up rice back onto her plate.

"It's okay," Memo told her. "I can't roll my *R*s, either."

"Even though it's easy," Neida said.

"Arrrrrrrrrrrrrrroz."

"Just pretend there's a buzzing bumblebee in your mouth," Mari suggested.

"Ew," Dina said. "No."

"Then try pretending that your tongue is a hummingbird's wing," Mari said.

"Yuck!" Dina said, but she tried anyway. This time it worked. The word "arroz" rolled off of her tongue perfectly.

Everyone cheered—even Memo, though it kind of hurt to cheer. He had been trying to turn his tongue into a hummingbird wing ever since he was Dina's age. It never worked. His Rs refused to roll. He felt like Spanish was magic, and he just didn't have the talent for it. Like those magic words had chosen his sisters, but not him. Like he was the Unchosen One.

Memo swallowed that disappointed feeling

along with a mouthful of plantain. He tried to cheer himself up by thinking about the Sorcery tournament. The grand prize was a treasure chest filled with rare and powerful cards like "Volcanic Hiccup" and "Telepathic Earworm." Memo wanted those spells. He wanted to feel like magic had chosen him.

"Hey, Dad," he said. "You can still drive Theo and me to MagiCon next weekend, right?"

Dad froze with his fork halfway to his mouth.

"Oops," he said.

## Chapter 4
# The Curse of Forgetting

"I'm sorry, hijo," Dad said. "I just can't do it."

He listed a whole bunch of work reasons and baby reasons why he needed to stay home next weekend. Those reasons all sounded like gibberish to Memo. He couldn't hear or understand them over the hurricane-like sound of his own crushing disappointment.

"Mom?" he pleaded.

"Wish I could," she said, "but I have to run

at least four different meetings and also zib-bidy boopa lo ort."

More excuses. More gibberish. Memo looked at his eldest sister. "Mari?"

"Can't," Mari said. "I've got a field hockey game next Saturday. Plus fleem and fibble."

Memo looked at his grandmother. Lala looked back with a sad smile and shrugged. He didn't know how much of the conversation she had understood. Maybe it sounded like gibberish to her, too. He did know that she couldn't drive to the city. Or anywhere else. Lala didn't have an American driver's license.

He and Theo had been looking forward to MagiCon all year. Now they had no way to get there. All of this felt like an evil curse, and Memo didn't know how to break it.

After dinner Memo fed the family pets, but he was so distracted that he almost let a bunch of live crickets escape from Falkor's cage.

Falkor was a bearded dragon lizard. He couldn't fly or breathe fire, but he did puff up his neck whenever he got grumpy about something. That made it look like he had a beard.

Memo felt like he also had a beard of grumpiness.

He watched the pet dragon chase crickets and crunch them without mercy.

Then he heard singing.

The sound was coming from Lala's room. Her door was partly open.

Memo stood in the hallway and listened.

His grandmother was singing an old Cuban song called "Guantanamera." He only knew what bits and pieces of it meant, but he thought that it was about missing home. He also knew that it was Lala's favorite.

*"Yo soy un mujer sincera*
*de donde crecen las palmas,*
*y antes de morir yo quiero*
*echar mis versos del alma.*
*Guantanameraaaaaaaaa . . ."*

He clomped up to his own bedroom and shut the door. Then he made up new lyrics to the song, just in case the tune was its own kind of magic spell.

*"I am a poor sorcerer*
*with no ride into town.*

*Dad can't be our driver*
*He flaked and let us down.*
*Now we can't go to the convention,*
*We can't go to the*
*conveeeeeeeeentioooooooooooon . . ."*

Singing didn't fix anything, but it did make him feel a little bit better—at least until he realized that tomorrow he would have to tell Theo the bad news.

## Chapter 5
# Magic Potions

Monday mornings at Memo's house were always messy.

Mom and Dad passed baby Ana back and forth while they got ready for work. Both of them worked from home. The actual "work" seemed to be mostly video meetings with coworkers scattered all over the world. Sometimes baby Ana got to be part of those meetings, but usually not.

Mari and Neida scarfed down some cereal and slurped tall glasses of café con leche. ("Café con leche" meant "coffee with milk." In this case, it meant a teeeeeeeeny bit of coffee, a lot of warm milk, and a whole bunch of sugar.)

"Can I try some?" Memo asked. All of the older Castillos treated coffee like some kind of magic potion. Today he would need all of the bonus help that he could get.

Lala looked up from her own cup and said something in Spanish.

"She says you're too young," Mari translated. Then his two older sisters ran outside to catch the bus to the high school.

Memo, Dina, and Lala all walked to Curiosity Academy together. It wasn't far away. Memo and Dina could have handled the walk by themselves, but Lala insisted on going with them.

*Maybe she thinks I'm going to break my other leg just by crossing the street*, Memo thought, *or maybe she doesn't trust me to look after Dina.* That was annoying. He was old enough to mind his little sister, and he was definitely old enough to cross the street.

They brought Dina to the preschool entrance, which had its own little fenced-in playground. Then Memo and Lala walked around to the front of the building. Lala didn't say anything when they got there. Instead, she kissed Memo's forehead, turned around, and went home.

Theo met him outside the front doors, just like always.

*I need to tell you about our ride to the convention,*

Memo thought, *and how we don't have one anymore*.

He couldn't bring himself to say it out loud.

Both of them took deep breaths like they were about to leap into a swimming pool.

"Ready?" Theo asked.

"Born ready," Memo said.

They pushed through the open doors and into the joyfully loud, crowded hallways of Curiosity Academy.

Theo didn't like crowds very much, and really loud crowds were the worst kind. Memo didn't like pushing through all of that hub-bub with crutches, and the busy stairway was especially awkward. Both boys headed for the elevator rather than the stairs.

The school elevator was new. It was shiny. It was also very slow. The doors took a long

time to open, and a long time to close once Theo and Memo were inside. Then it was finally quiet.

"Whew," Theo said. "MagiCon is probably going to be loud and crowded, but I have a plan! I made a special noise-cancelling part of my costume."

Memo said nothing.

"We still have Sorcery practice at Doomscroll this afternoon, right?" Theo asked.

Memo nodded.

Doomscroll Comics was one of their favorite places in the world. It had oodles of comics and books (of course), fantastical masks and costumes (like pointy elf ears, which Memo would need for his own costume, if he got a chance to wear it), and several shelves of games (including Sorcery). It even had a big plastic crate of used and tattered Sorcery cards, just for practice.

"We are going to win the tournament," Theo said.

*Not if we can't find a ride*, Memo thought.

The elevator slooooooooooooooowly inched its way up to the second floor.

## Chapter 6

# The Secret Garden

Memo and Theo got to the classroom last. That often happened. Crutches and elevators slowed them down. Memo tried not to feel embarrassed about it.

"Welcome, everyone!" said Mrs. Z. Today she wore glass earrings that looked like tiny planets with swirling clouds. "Emma, tell us which holiday we are going to celebrate."

Emma stood up and played a few notes on her recorder. "Today is National Dessert Day!"

Memo liked the sound of that.

"Today is *also* our first day working in the new Outdoor Learning Center," Mrs. Z said. "It's a beautiful day, so we're going outside to plant bulbs in the garden. I brought cupcakes to celebrate both occasions, since we shouldn't expect Poppy to do *all* of our classroom baking. The cake is meant to look like dirt, and the green frosting like little sprouting plants, but I promise that they don't taste like dirt. They taste like chocolate."

"Do we get to eat them now?" Ayana asked.

Mrs. Z shook her head. "No, not now. Dessert comes at the end of a meal, so we'll have cupcakes at the end of the day. Besides, I find that sugar makes it hard for me to focus on classroom stuff. First it gives me too much energy . . ." She waved her arms around over her head. ". . . and then all of that energy crashes and I want to take a nap." She let both arms flop to her sides. "We have lots to do today before cupcake time. Let's start with the Daily Scribble."

# The Daily Scribble
## for Monday, october 14

what do you think the world will be like 100 years from now?

The whole class started scribbling.

We'll hear radio signals from space and start talking to people on other planets. Then we'll invent a universal translator,

*just like the one on Star Trek, and the whole galaxy will finally make sense.*
*Everyone will understand everyone else.*

The five-minute timer dinged.

"Who would like to share?" Mrs. Z asked.

Rohan hoped that every rooftop in the world would have solar panels in a hundred years.

Synclaire said that there would be cities on Mars.

Mars insisted that mutant vampires would rule the world, and that human survivors would mostly eat grasshoppers.

"Grasshoppers are good sources of protein," Mrs. Z pointed out. "Also, they taste kind of nutty."

Later they went to work at the Outdoor

Learning Center. Memo thought that the trowels looked like daggers.

Mrs. Z seemed to read his mind. "Garden tools are not for dueling," she whispered from right behind him.

Memo nodded. "No duels," he promised.

His cast made it tricky for Memo to reach the ground. He volunteered to sort bulbs at one of the outdoor tables rather than crouching down to dig in the dirt.

Lala's favorite song was stuck in his head. He couldn't remember most of the actual lyrics, so he made up a few more of his own and sang to himself while he worked.

*"I wonder if trees can talk.*
*What do these plants have to say?*
*Maybe they wish they could walk*
*Instead of staying in one place . . ."*

"Good," said Mrs. Z. "Plants like it when you sing to them."

Memo stopped, embarrassed.

At the end of the school day Memo and Theo took the elevator back downstairs.

"You have crumbs on your face," Theo said.

"So do you," Memo said.

Both of them used their shirt sleeves as napkins to clean their faces. The cupcakes had been delicious, and they didn't taste like garden dirt.

The elevator finally got to the first floor and dinged.

"Ready?" Theo asked.

"Born ready," Memo said.

The doors opened. The two of them pushed

through the crowded, joyful hubbub of school dismissal. Memo accidentally bumped into Wyatt.

"Sorry," they said at the same time, and then both of them laughed.

Lala and Dina were waiting outside.

"Go ahead and walk home without me," Memo said to his sister and grandma. "Theo and I are hanging out at Doomscroll Comics. I'll be home before dinner, okay?"

Lala said something that sounded like Very Important Instructions before she took Dina's hand and started walking home.

"What did that mean?" Theo asked.

"Don't be late for dinner?" Memo guessed.

*I have no idea,* he thought, *but I don't want to admit that I can't understand her. And I also don't want to admit that we don't have a ride to the convention anymore because my dad forgot.*

*Just like you said he would. I do need to tell you. Soon. But maybe not right now? Maybe I can find another way. Then I'll be able to say "Ta-da! Problem solved!" before you even know that there's a problem.*

Memo watched his grandmother and his little sister cross the street.

He got an idea.

Lala couldn't drive, but maybe she could still help them get downtown.

## Chapter 7
# The Song of Victory

Theo was not sure about the new plan. "We have to take the city bus?"

"It'll be great," Memo said. "Lala uses it all the time. She can show us how to get to the convention center. And this way we won't have to worry about my dad forgetting all about it."

"Because he already forgot," Theo said.

"Exactly," Memo said.

Theo shrugged. "As long as we can still get

to MagiCon, I do not really care how. Unless we tried to ride on unicycles. I would definitely crash if we did that."

"No unicycles," Memo promised. "I've got one broken leg already."

He felt relieved to have a plan. There was still hope. He just needed to convince Lala to go with them. Memo had no idea how to explain a science fiction and fantasy convention to his grandmother, especially when the two of them didn't really speak the same language.

He tried not to think about that.

The two friends arrived at Doomscroll Comics.

"Welcome, gentlemen!" Carla Brandon shouted from behind the counter. Her parents owned the store, which meant that she won the My Parents Have the Best Job in the Entire World Award. Carla usually worked a shift at Doomscroll right after school. "Are you here for Sorcery cards? Shopping for convention costumes? Or hoping to read the latest team-up between Squirrel Girl and Miles Morales?"

"All three!" said Memo.

"Just the Sorcery cards for me, please, and thank you," Theo said.

"Excellent," Carla said. "Memo, what do you need costume-wise?"

"Pointy ears," he told her.

Carla pointed. "Right over there, near the capes and cloaks. Theo, the crate of slightly used spells awaits you at the game table."

Theo practically danced over to a folding table at the back of the store, sat down near the crate, and started to pick out his favorite kinds of spells.

Memo paused by a display case next to

the cash register. Rare and powerful Sorcery cards were locked inside that case. The best one was "The Sword of the Mountain King." It cost as much as a brand-new bicycle.

The one thing that Memo didn't love about his favorite card game was how expensive it could get. Players who spent a ton of money on Sorcery packs and very rare cards got to use all of the most powerful spells in a duel. Luckily, Doomscroll let Memo and Theo have first dibs on used cards.

Memo searched through the costumes until he found a pair of pointy ears. They were even the same color as the rest of him, which he appreciated.

"What are you planning to be?" Carla asked. "Vulcan?"

"Elf," Memo said. "How about you? What's your costume this year?"

"Vera Gallant the Werewolf Tamer!" Carla announced proudly. "She's the main character of my favorite science fiction circus comic. Both the artist and the writer are going to be at the convention on Saturday, so I'm going to get them to sign my copy of the first issue." Carla took her costumes—what convention people called "cosplay"—seriously. She had probably been working on her Vera Gallant costume all year. "Are the two of you playing in the Sorcery tournament?"

"Yes," Theo said without looking up from the piles of cards.

"Totally," Memo agreed. "Are you?"

Carla shook her head. "I'm in the Geeky Karaoke Competition."

"The what?" Memo had never heard of it.

"You sing a famous song while listening to the music," she explained, "just like with regular karaoke. But you also have to make up new and geeky lyrics. Listen. *This* is how it's done." She stood on the counter next to the cash register and sang:

*"And the werewolves gonna bite bite bite*
*bite bite,*
*They are creatures of the night night night*
*night night,*
*But their curse will never fright fright*
*fright fright fright,*
*'Cause I can break it all, break it all!"*

Theo clapped. Memo cheered.

"Thank you, thank you," Carla said as she climbed down. "Will either of you try singing instead of Sorcery?"

"Nope," Theo said.

"Definitely not," Memo agreed.

Carla grinned. "You're missing out!"

Two more classmates showed up at the store: Mars and Emma. Mars waved on his way to the latest issue of *Mighty Monsters*. Emma came over to say hi.

"Can I sign your cast?" she asked Memo.

"Sure!" He sat next to Theo and propped up his broken leg on another chair. "Unless you'd rather draw a dragon?"

She drew a dragon with sharp teeth and butterfly wings.

Then the front door opened and Josh Harkan stepped inside.

"Welcome to Doomscroll," Carla said without enthusiasm.

Josh was a fifth grader at Curiosity Academy, and he swaggered around like he was even older.

Memo and Theo both tried to ignore him.

It's difficult to ignore someone when they loom over you and smirk.

"Silly kids," Josh said. "You'll never build a killer Sorcery deck with those old, used, reject cards."

"Do not mess with champion sorcerers," Theo said without looking up, "for we might turn you into a tadpole."

Memo felt like breathing fire. "We're going to win," he said. "At the tournament. We're going to beat you and laugh over the ashes of your cards."

Josh's smirk got even smirkier. "Carla," he said, "I need ten of the newest, shiniest Sorcery packs."

"Ten?" she asked. "Really?"

"Really," Josh insisted. "I have a tournament to win this weekend."

Ten packs cost *a lot*. This was how Josh

Harkan had won the tournament last year. He bought a huge pile of shiny new cards like money didn't matter to him.

He tapped the display case. "I'll also take 'The Sword of the Mountain King.'"

"You're kidding," Carla said.

"I'm not kidding." Josh paid with his own debit card, stuck the new spells in his pocket, and waved to Memo on his way out the door. "Bye, kids."

"I hope you really do beat that guy," Emma muttered.

"We will," Theo said. "Because I just found a card with a picture of Memo on it. Look!"

Memo tried to reach for the one Theo held.

"Don't move!" Emma said. "I'm not done drawing yet."

Theo got up from the table and showed them. The card was called "Sing a Song of

Victory," and the elf in the picture really did look like Memo.

Carla glanced at the card and whistled. "You need to keep that! Look, he's singing. This obviously means that you're going to enter the karaoke contest. It's destiny."

"Nope," Theo said. "It is obviously a sign that we're going to win the Sorcery tournament. It has the word 'victory' in the title, see? New and shiny cards are not important. We just need to find a bunch of old ones that work together best."

Memo stuck the card in his pocket. "Thanks, Carla," he said. "No karaoke for me, though."

"Suit yourself," Carla said, "but I think you'd be great."

Memo blushed. He did love to sing. He just didn't want anyone else to hear.

"Choose your spells, sorcerer!" Theo said.

Memo picked a few cards and he and Theo started to play.

He needed to practice.

He needed to defeat Josh Harkan—even though the fifth grader had just spent a fortune on a bazillion shiny new cards.

But first of all, he needed to convince Lala to come to the convention.

## Chapter 8

# The Jabberwock

"Did you ask her yet?" Theo asked. It was Wednesday morning, and the school elevator was climbing up to the second floor at the speed of sleepy slugs.

"Not yet," Memo said.

"We are already halfway to Saturday," Theo reminded him.

"I know!" Memo had tried to talk to Lala the night before, but she looked so much like a mysterious queen who only spoke Elvish that he just couldn't think of what to say. "I'll ask today. Right after school."

The elevator finally dinged and opened.

"Welcome, everyone!" said Mrs. Z. Today her earrings were made out of old typewriter keys. She had a question mark on her left ear and an exclamation point on her right. "Emma, what holiday are we celebrating?"

Emma stood up and grinned. "Today is National Dictionary Day!"

"Excellent," said Mrs. Z. "We'll start our dictionary-themed celebrations with the Daily Scribble. Settle in and get started."

# The Daily Scribble
## for Wednesday, October 16

The poem "Jabberwocky" by Lewis Carroll begins and ends with these four lines:

'Twas brillig, and the slithy toves
Did gyre and gimble in the wabe
All mimsy were the borogoves,
And the mome raths outgrabe.

Invent a dictionary definition for one
of these imaginary words.

Memo started scribbling. He didn't stop to
think about it first, because he didn't think
that thinking would help. *Those words make no
sense!* his brain would say. Memo ignored his
brain and just started writing.

Brillig (adjective): stormy weather filled
with choruses of singing ghosts.

"Would anyone like to share?" Mrs. Z asked
when the timer dinged.

Thunder raised her hand. "Well," she said, "I think that mome raths are animals that move around in herds and have really long tongues like giraffes."

Next Mrs. Z called on Sebastian. "'Slithy' describes the icky feeling that I've got right now."

"Why do you feel slithy?" Mrs. Z wondered.

"Because dictionary definitions are supposed to be *real*," he said. "Not just silly and made up."

Mrs. Z smiled. "That's fair," she said. "It might feel less slithy to think about where words come from. Somebody had to make them up. Why not you? Why not now?"

Carlota went next. "Borogoves are a kind of tropical tree," she said. "They can walk on their roots, and talk to each other, and put on plays when nobody else is there to hear them."

Memo knew Carlota's family was from Cuba and Puerto Rico. Both islands were tropical places. Memo wondered if talking trees knew how to roll their *R*s. He wondered if Carlota knew how to speak Spanish. Mrs. Z definitely did. She would chat in rapid Spanish with Memo's parents whenever they saw each other, and Memo would always pretend that he understood. It always felt like he *should* understand.

He wished for a Sorcery card called "Speak the Languages of Your Family." Maybe then he could tell Lala all about the convention and explain why it would be amazing.

"Anyone else?" Mrs. Z asked.

Memo felt slithy, so he didn't raise his hand.

That slithy feeling stuck with him through the rest of the day—all the way up to the moment when he knocked on the door of his grandmother's room. She was humming "Guantanamera" to herself.

"Hi, Lala," Memo said. "Can you help me with my costume? Um, ayúdame?" He was pretty sure that meant "help me."

Lala waved him in and looked at the costume. Then she asked a question. Memo loved the sound of it, but he could only guess what it meant.

"I'm going to be an elf," Memo said. "Here's the pointy rubber ears, see? Theo and I thought about dressing up as dragons, but those costume plans got too complicated. So now I'm an elf, and I need to hide my cast. Maybe we use this scrap of cloth?"

He took a long piece of brown fabric and started to wrap it around the cast.

Lala took a sewing kit out of a drawer and helped stitch the fabric in place. Now the cast looked like an old, tattered bandage instead. Memo thought it looked great.

"I was also thinking," he said, "that maybe you could come with us? To the science fiction and fantasy convention? Theo and I can't go alone, but maybe you could show us how to take the bus downtown? You don't have to wear a costume. But you can wear a costume if you want to. Maybe?"

Lala scrunched her eyebrows together. She looked a bit confused. *This isn't working*, Memo thought.

He heard his sisters in the kitchen and called out for help. "Neida! Mari! Is anyone out there?"

Neida stuck her head in the doorway. "What?" she asked around a mouthful of potato chips.

"Can you ask Lala to bring Theo and me to MagiCon on Saturday?" Memo asked. "And show us how to use the bus?"

Neida rattled off some Spanish while still eating chips, which made the words sound extra muddled to Memo.

Lala's answer sounded long and complicated, but Neida gave a very short translation. "She says okay."

Memo and Lala both smiled nervously. How was the trip to the city going to work out if they couldn't really understand each other?

# Chapter 9
# Welcoming Worlds

An elf, a cyborg, and a queen sat together on
a bus.

The elf wore a green cloak and one leather
boot. His right foot was wrapped in a whole
bunch of brown and green cloth to hide his
plaster cast, and he used a staff instead of
crutches. The staff looked like something
that the elf could use to cast mighty spells,
but it was a little awkward to carry on a bus.
He tried to keep it from bonking anyone

whenever the bus drove over a bump in the road.

The cyborg sat next to the window and fidgeted with a small model of a spaceship. He wore a helmet made out of plastic and foil, which covered up his noise-canceling headphones. The headphones made it easier to ride on a loud and crowded bus. They would also help him with the loud and crowded convention.

The queen held a wooden cane with a silver handle. She wore an elegant black and silver dress, and frowned when the elf's staff bonked into the side of her head.

"¡Lo siento!" said the elf, because *I'm sorry* was one of the few things that he knew how to say in Spanish.

"Cuidado, duende," said the queen, which meant *Be careful, elf.*

The bus arrived at the convention center.

"Ready?" the cyborg asked.

"Born ready," the elf said, and he almost believed it.

Memo, Theo, and Lala found the convention hall and stepped into another world—into *lots* of other worlds, all of them smooshed together. Knights chatted with astronauts. Wizards sipped coffee with droids and airbenders. An owlbear wore a beautiful ballgown. Every universe was invited, and all of them belonged.

"Wow!" Memo said. The awkward, hourlong bus ride had been absolutely worth it.

"I love this place," Theo agreed. "Okay, the first thing we need to do is register for the

Sorcery tournament. Then we should go to the Goblin Market. After that is Teatime for Time Travelers, and after that . . ."

"After that we'll just figure it out as we go," Memo said. He wanted to explore without a schedule or a plan.

"Okay." Theo pointed and charged. "To the tournament!"

"Come on, Lala!" Memo said.

His grandmother glanced around her at the superhero costumes and cardboard robot suits. She seemed a little nervous.

"It's okay," he told her. "This place is great! Anything's possible here, and all of it's happening at once."

Lala gave him a look. *That is exactly my problem*, said her look. *Everything is happening at once, and I don't understand any of it.*

Memo took her hand and led her through the overlapping worlds.

"Did you bring 'Sing a Song of Victory'?" Theo asked once they got to the tournament sign-up table.

"Of course," Memo said.

"Good," Theo said. "That card is the perfect luck charm."

"It's a bit embarrassing, though," Memo admitted.

"Why?" Theo asked.

"Because the picture looks a lot like me," Memo said.

"Which is what makes it great!" Theo said. "And you are dressed up like an elf right now. In public. What is embarrassing about looking just as awesome as the picture on a Sorcery card?"

Memo shrugged. "Maybe because the elf on the card is singing?"

"You sing all the time," Theo pointed out. "You just try to hide it."

Josh Harkan joined the line right behind them. He looked even taller than usual, and his dark hair was slicked back. Memo couldn't tell whether or not Josh was wearing a vampire costume because Josh usually looked like a vampire.

"Hello, little sorcerers," the older boy said with his usual smirk. "Good luck in the tournament." He said it in a way that sounded more like, *I hope your spells all backfire in your face.*

"Same to you," Memo told him, though he meant to say, *I hope that baby dragons set your socks on fire.*

After they signed up for the tournament, Theo marched them toward the Goblin Market—a huge room filled with folding tables and lots of fantastical things for sale.

Memo had been saving up his allowance, but he wasn't sure what he wanted to buy.

He overheard a gaggle of zombies talk about glow-in-the-dark dice at the ThunderGnome table.

He saw a whole flock of robots admiring jewelry at the Atlantean Artifacts table.

He watched while an alien with a huge purple mask argued about the price of used comics at the Doomscroll table.

"Do you think this would be a good place for people from other planets to visit Earth for the first time?" Memo asked Theo. "Maybe they would blend in with all the costumes, and no one would take them seriously."

"Or maybe *everyone* would take them seriously," Theo said. "Science fiction fans have had lots of practice talking to people like that guy." He pointed at the alien with the purple mask.

Memo wasn't so sure. "But what if they use smells to talk? Or send messages by changing the color of their hair?"

"We would still figure it out," Theo said.

The big purple guy bought some comics and then wandered away from the Doomscroll table. Memo and Theo pushed through the crowd to say hi. The whole Brandon family was there. Carla's costume looked exactly like the cover art for *Vera Gallant, Werewolf Tamer #1*.

"Gentlemen!" Carla said. "I was just headed over to the main stage. Are you *absolutely sure* that you don't want to ditch the card tournament and come sing karaoke instead?"

"We're sure," Memo said.

"Very," Theo said.

"Then wish me luck," Carla said. "Not that I'll need it. Bye!"

Mrs. Brandon waved Memo and Theo closer to the table. "Are you boys here all by yourselves?" she asked.

"We're here with my abuela," Memo said.

He looked around, expecting to see Lala right behind him.

She wasn't there.

Lala had disappeared.

## Chapter 10
# Universal Translation

First Memo and Theo searched the whole Goblin Market. Then they looked for Lala in the hallways and lobby. After that they asked for help at the help desk, but the Starfleet captain behind the desk wasn't very helpful.

"We can put out an announcement and ask your grandmother to come find you right here," he said. "What's her name?"

"Dolores Castillo," Memo told him. "She doesn't speak English, though."

"Oh," said the captain.

"Do you speak Spanish?" Memo asked hopefully.

"No," said the captain. "Do you?"

"Sure he does," Theo said.

Memo closed his eyes, feeling slithier than he had ever felt before.

He thought about trying to make an announcement, in Spanish, to every single person in the convention hall.

The few words that he knew disappeared from his brain.

"No," he admitted. "Nope, nope, nope. I don't. Not really."

Theo looked very confused. "What?"

"Sometimes I understand a little bit," Memo said, "and sometimes I pretend to know more, just because it seems like I *should* be able to. But my family mostly speaks English. The

rest sounds like magic spells to someone who can't do any magic."

Theo didn't say anything.

"I'm sorry," Memo whispered. "Sorry that I sorta lied."

His best friend grinned. "It is okay. Really. My Korean is terrible."

Memo's slithy feeling faded a little.

The Starfleet captain awkwardly cleared his throat behind the help desk. "It's a shame that universal translators aren't real," he said. "Then we could talk to whales and dolphins. I've always wanted to do that."

"Me too," Theo said.

They left the unhelpful help desk.

Memo felt prickles of panic in the middle of his chest. "We need to find Lala. She came here to look after us, but we forgot to look after her."

"We cannot play in the tournament without a grown-up there to sponsor us," Theo said.

"And she'll be worried," Memo pointed out. "I wish I could cast a spell of finding. Then I'd summon a whole bunch of fireflies to show us the way. Or the floor would light up and tell us where we needed to go. Or else I would just *sense* Lala, like a compass trying to find north. I'd know that she's somewhere over *there*." He pointed with his staff.

"Do you really think she is somewhere over there?" Theo asked.

"No," Memo said.

"Me neither," Theo said, "and we do not have much time to look before the tournament begins. We are already going to miss Teatime for Time Travelers! I wish we could use a time machine to repeat this whole day and tell our past selves where your grandmother is."

Memo tried to come up with a plan that didn't involve either magic spells or time travel.

Lala was lost somewhere in a huge crowd of goblins and robots.

He didn't know how to find her.

He didn't think that she would be able to find him.

Then he heard familiar singing in the distance:

*"And the werewolves gonna bite bite bite bite bite,*
*They are creatures of the night night night night night,*
*But their curse will never fright fright fright fright fright,*
*'Cause I can break it all, break it all!"*

"I've got an idea," Memo told Theo. "It's either the best or the worst idea that I've ever had. Come on!"

## Chapter 11

# The Ballad of Memo Castillo

They followed Carla's voice to the main stage.

She finished her song. The crowd roared applause.

Memo found the sign-up sheet.

"There's an empty slot right now," said a volunteer with bright blue face paint. "Someone else just chickened out. You can take it if you want."

Memo took it. His staff and cast made loud

*ka-thunking* noises when he climbed up the ramp and onto the stage. A live band of musicians waited for him.

"What are we playing?" asked the lead guitarist. He wore a top hat with a goblin puppet peeking out of it.

"Do you know 'Guantanamera'?" Memo asked.

"Claro que sí," said the guitarist. "Are you ready?"

"Born ready," Memo said, even though he didn't believe it.

The whole band started playing Lala's favorite song.

*She'll hear us*, Memo thought. *She'll follow the music. She'll follow my voice. But first I need to start singing. In front of an audience. A really big audience full of trolls and superheroes.*

This was terrifying. He closed his eyes. That

made the stage fright feel even worse, so he opened his eyes and faced his audience.

Theo and Carla waved at him from the wings.

Memo lifted the microphone and desperately tried to make up a whole bunch of new lyrics. The first two lines popped into his head.

*"I am an elf from an island*
*Where trees are taller than towers . . ."*

"Louder!" shouted a robot at the back of the crowd.

Memo sang louder.

*"I am an elf from an island,*
*Where trees are taller than towers,*
*And I hope that these notes*
*Have queen-summoning powers."*

Luckily, Memo remembered how to say *Where are you?* in both Spanish and English by the time he got to the chorus.

> *"Where are you, Lala?*
> *¿Dónde estás, mi abuela?*
> *Where are you, Lalaaaaaaaaa?*
> *¿Dónde estás, mi abuelaaaaaaaaaa?"*

He still didn't see her anywhere, so now he needed to sing another verse.

> *"My queen is haunting this place,*
> *Where words are strange to her ears.*
> *Where in this crowd is her face?*
> *Will my own voice guide her here?"*

This time the whole audience sang the chorus along with him.

*"Where are you, Lala?*

*¿Dónde estás, mi abuela?*

*Where are you, Lalaaaaaaaaa?"*

Then he saw Lala in the back of the room, grinning a huge grin to hear her grandson sing. "¡Estoy aquí, mi nietoooooo!" she sang back to him.

Everybody cheered.

## Chapter 12
# The Return of the Queen

"That was amazing!" Carla cheered when Memo got down from the stage. "See, I told you that karaoke was your destiny."

"We were both right," Theo said. "His destiny is *also* waiting for him at the Sorcery tournament. As my teammate. In about two minutes!"

Memo couldn't hurry quite as fast with a staff as he could with crutches, but he did the best he could. "Come on, Lala!" he said. "I know that you don't understand why, but we have to hurry!"

"I do understand," she said.

Memo stopped hurrying. "What?"

"You have a . . . special card game?" Lala said slowly and carefully, thinking hard about every word. "You want to win . . . and also to beat that boy who looks like a vampire."

Memo stared at her.

"Ay," Lala said. "Don't look at me like that. I understand some English. Just like you with español. And I can say a little bit. Just like you. But I'm also embarrassed. I wish I knew more. So I don't usually say very much. Just like you."

Memo hugged her.

"Time to goooooooooooooo!" Theo called from down the hallway.

The Sorcery tournament began.

Memo and Theo matched spells against Josh Harkan and his partner, the alien with the purple mask.

Josh wasn't much of a team player. He kept trying to show off all by himself rather than working with his teammate. Theo banished Josh's army of skeletons, and then Memo cast a hurricane made out of whispered wishes to block the Sword of the Mountain King.

They won.

It was glorious.

"Good game," Josh muttered when he left the table.

"Well played!" said the purple guy with much more enthusiasm. "You two are a dynamic duo."

Memo and Theo kept on playing well for the rest of the tournament, because they were a fantastic team, but they didn't win the grand prize. Instead, they lost their very last match to a pair of mermaids.

Theo was still thrilled. "We won second place! That comes with a slightly smaller treasure chest of brand-new cards."

Memo didn't mind losing to the mermaids, either, because his abuela was laughing at her favorite costumes and singing softly to herself.

A gray-haired Vulcan in a flowing robe walked by.

Lala held up her hand in greeting. "Viva una vida larga y prospere."

The Vulcan answered, "Live long and prosper."

Memo stared. Lala winked at him. "I watch a lot of *Star Trek* dubbed into Spanish. Mr. Spock is my favorite."

They all went back to the Goblin Market,

where Memo used his allowance money to buy a huge, goofy, glowing, battery-powered crown from Atlantean Artifacts.

He offered the crown to Lala.

"Here," Memo said. "This will make it easier to find you if you get lost again."

Lala accepted the crown. "Gracias, mi querido duende."

Memo bowed as best he could, which was tricky in a cast.

"You're welcome, my queen."

© Alice Dodge

# About the Author

**WILLIAM ALEXANDER** mostly writes unrealisms for young readers. He won the National Book Award for his first novel, *Goblin Secrets*, and the Earphones Award for reading the audiobook. When he was very young, he believed that his Cuban-American family came from the lost island of Atlantis, which turned out to be untrue.

In third grade, William dressed up as a wizard to deliver a book report on *The Hobbit*. The fake beard was very itchy.

**willalex.net**

© Kat Fajardo

# About the Illustrator

**KAT FAJARDO** (they/she) received a Pura Belpré Honor for Illustration for their first graphic novel, *Miss Quinces* (published in Spanish as *Srta. Quinces*). Born and raised in New York City, Kat now lives in Austin, Texas, with their pups, Mac and Roni.

**katfajardo.com**

# The Creators of

The **Kids** in Mrs. Z's Class

William Alexander

Tracey Baptiste

Martha Brockenbrough

Christine Day

Lamar Giles

Karina Yan Glaser

Mike Jung

Hena Khan

Rajani LaRocca

Kyle Lukoff

Kekla Magoon

Meg Medina

Kate Messner

Olugbemisola Rhuday-Perkovich

Eliot Schrefer

Laurel Snyder

Linda Urban

# Read on for a preview of Book Five in the series,

# *Wyatt Hill's Best Friend Is a Lizard*

## BY **ELIOT SCHREFER**

## Chapter 1

# What Makes You Unique, Wyatt Hill?

Wyatt Hill noticed that something strange happened each day at recess: Even though boys and girls mixed together in Mrs. Z's classroom, as soon as they put their winter coats on and went outside to play, the boys headed in one direction and the girls in another. It was like there was some unwritten rule.

To get to the field where the boys hung out, Wyatt first had to walk by the paved area where the girls played hopscotch. Today, Fia tossed a nub of purple chalk on the number four and hopped along wildly on one foot, while Ayana cheered her on and Ruthie sang an encouraging song. It looked like a lot of fun, but boys didn't play over there.

Patting his backpack to make sure Lizzie was secure, Wyatt trudged over to the boys' field and stood beside Memo and Theo. They watched Rohan give a running start and kick the grass, sending a clod of dirt flying. "Morning, guys," Wyatt said.

"Morning, Wyatt," Memo said, watching the clod fall back down. He scrunched his eyes shut as it sprayed bits of dirt over all of them.

Wyatt looked over at the hopscotch game, where Emma was jumping over a piece of pink chalk on the number two. Then he looked back at the dirt of the field. He stuck his hands deep in his pockets as he watched Adam take his turn. The boys were seeing if any of them could kick the grass hard enough to send a clump of it into the air. It had been their recess game all week. But Wyatt didn't really want to kick dirt. In fact, he couldn't figure out why anyone thought kicking dirt was fun.

He listened to Memo and Theo discuss the fantasy convention they went to last month. Wyatt hadn't gone, so he didn't have much to say about it. He had a mental conversation with Lizzie, in his backpack. It was a big day for her—the semifinals for the Reptile World Cup.

Then Wyatt felt a tug on his sleeve. It was Ruthie. "You need to come with me, Wyatt Hill," she declared.

"Me?" Wyatt asked. "You want to talk to *me*?"

"Yes, you," Ruthie said.

Ruthie was often the center of all the fun

on the girls' side of recess. From what Wyatt had observed, it was usually Ruthie who came up with new versions of hopscotch, like giggle-hop or everyone-has-to-step-on-three-at-once, and one time she'd even gotten all the girls to reenact a music video, complete with costumes they'd brought from home. Today Ruthie's entire outfit was fluorescent green, except for her shiny black shoes. There was no saying no to her in normal situations, and especially not when she was dressed like a highlighter.

"Are you really going with her?" Memo asked. He looked stunned and a little impressed. "I guess you've been summoned. Good luck!"

Theo solemnly laid a hand on Wyatt's shoulder. "May the gods be with you."

# The **Kids** in Mrs. **Z's Class**